D1270872

First Day of School

FRANKLIN PIERCE COLLEGE
LIBRARY
RINDGE, NEW HAMPSHIRE

CURR
PZ
7
.0975
Fi
1993

For Emily and Anna

PUFFIN PIED PIPER BOOKS
Published by the Penguin Group
Penguin Books USA Inc., 375 Hudson Street, New York, New York 10014, U.S.A.
Penguin Books Ltd, 27 Wrights Lane, London W8 5TZ, England
Penguin Books Australia Ltd, Ringwood, Victoria, Australia
Penguin Books Canada Ltd, 10 Alcorn Avenue, Toronto, Ontario, Canada M4V 3B2
Penguin Books (N.Z.) Ltd, 182-190 Wairau Road, Auckland 10, New Zealand
Penguin Books Ltd, Registered Offices: Harmondsworth, Middlesex, England

First published in the United States 1983
by Dial Books for Young Readers
A Division of Penguin Books USA Inc.

Published in Great Britain by Walker Books, Inc.
Copyright © 1983 by Helen Oxenbury
All rights reserved
Library of Congress Catalog Card Number: 83-7452
Printed in Hong Kong
First Puffin Pied Piper Printing 1993
ISBN 0-14-054977-3
1 3 5 7 9 10 8 6 4 2
A Pied Piper Book is a registered trademark of
Dial Books for Young Readers, a division of Penguin Books USA Inc.,
® TM 1,163,686 and ® TM 1,054,312.

First Day of School

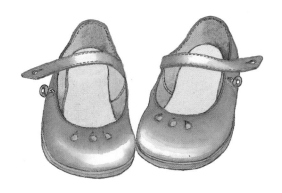

by Helen Oxenbury

A Puffin Pied Piper

"Time to get up! You don't want
to be late for your first day
of nursery school. And you can
wear your new shoes."

"Don't worry," Mommy said, "you'll
   make lots of new friends."
"I don't think I'm going to like
   it here," I said.

"Don't leave me, Mommy!"
"It's all right," the teacher said.
"Your mommy can stay for a while,
 if you want."

"This is Nora. She just hurt her knee.
Look! You have the same shoes on."

"I'll be back soon," Mommy said.
"Come on, you two," the teacher said.
"Let's pretend to be animals."

The teacher in the pink dress
read us a story. At snack time
I shared my raisins with Nora.

"Remember to wash your hands.
Then we'll sing some songs."

"See you tomorrow," said the teacher.
"Your mommies and daddies are waiting."

About the Author/Artist

Helen Oxenbury is internationally recognized as one of the finest children's book illustrators, with over thirty books to her credit, including *We're Going on a Bear Hunt* and *The Dragon of an Ordinary Family* (Dial) by Margaret Mahy. Her Very First Books®—five board books for toddlers—have been newly designed and reissued by Dial. According to *The Washington Post,* the books "will delight parents and entertain infants." *The Bulletin of the Center for Children's Books* applauded, "Fun, but more than that: These are geared to the toddler's interests and experiences." Ms. Oxenbury lives in London.